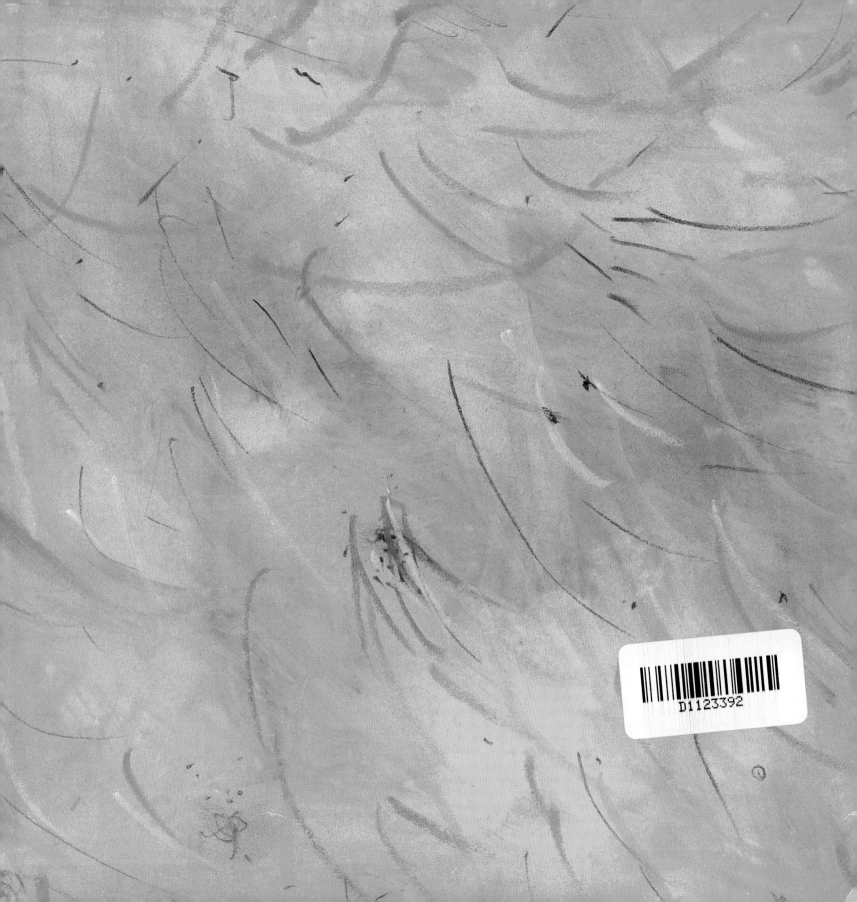

SMELLY BILL

Daniel Postgate

NorthSouth
BOOKS
New York

Bill the dog loved smelly things,
Like muddy ponds and rubbish bins.
Disgusting stuff he'd stick his snout in,
Sniff and snort and roll about in.

Because of this he had a bleak
And really quite unpleasant reek.
His family would cry,

'You stink!'

And try to get him in the sink.

But every time he'd get away
And live to stink another day.

A very smelly dog was Bill
And that's the way he stayed until...
One day his folks went to the beach

And left poor Bill **with**...

Great Aunt Bleach!

Now, Great Aunt Bleach just loved to clean.
On cleaning she was super keen.
With disinfectant, sponge and scrubber,
Vacuum, mop and gloves of rubber,
Great Aunt Bleach yelled,

'Tally-ho!'

And cleaned the house from tip to toe.

When every knife and fork was polished,
Every dirty mark abolished,
Great Aunt Bleach said,

'What's that smell?'

And that is when she spotted Bill.

Bleach twittered,
'Come on doggie-woo
It's **bathie-wathie**
time for you!'

Bleach was fast but Bill was faster.
Like a flash he dashed straight past her.
He knew exactly what to go for.

He scrambled underneath the sofa.

Just out of reach from Bleach he knew
That there was nothing she could do.
He snuggled up, that cheeky chap,
And settled down to take a nap.

When Bill woke up, before his eyes,
He saw a steak of mammoth size.
It was a lovely juicy thing.

It got him all a'dribbling.

Bill slid from underneath the seat
And sank his teeth into the meat.

It was a trick!

Bill had been fooled!

Bleach wound
**and pulled
and wound
and pulled,**

Until she had the smelly pet
Caught within her fishing net.

Then, with a laugh, Bleach filled the bath
Until the bath was brimming.
And, while she tipped in smelly stuff,
Bill heard the old girl singing:

'Oh, fizzy, lilac-scented balls,
Please hear the words I'm speaking;
Oh, apple blossom, lemon zest,
Cherry scrub, and all the rest,
Please do your very smelly best
To stop this beast from reeking.'

While Bleach was busy with her chants
Bill struggled from the net.
He saw the window, seized his chance
And out to freedom leapt.

Across the yard he had to race
To find the perfect hiding place.
He dug down deep, down deep within
A very smelly compost bin.

But oh, **too late!**
Bleach spotted him.

She wasted very little time
In climbing to the washing line,
Yelled, 'Bill, you will not
get away!'
And, like a great, plump bird of prey,
She swooped down to
the compost bin.

And landed right on top of him!

'Game over, doggie-woggie-woo.
It's **bathie-wathie** time for you!'

When they returned, the family
Were most surprised and pleased to see
A fluffy Bill, from nose to toes,
Smelling sweeter than a rose.

Bleach said,
'I do not like to boast,
But I'm the one
to thank.'

The children didn't get too close,

She absolutely stank!

For everyone at
Whitstable Day Nursery

Text and Illustrations copyright © 2006 by Daniel Postgate.
First published in Great Britain by Meadowside Children's Books.
New English edition copyright © 2007 by North-South Books Inc.

Published and distributed in the United States and Canada in 2007 by
North-South Books Inc., an imprint of NordSüd Verlag AG, Zürich, Switzerland.

Library of Congress Cataloging-in-Publication Data is available.
A CIP catalogue record for this book is available from The British Library.

ISBN-13: 978-0-7358-2135-4
ISBN-10: 0-7358-2135-6

3 5 7 9 10 8 6 4 2

Printed in Belgium